CW00819244

THE ADVENTURES OF SHAY MOUSE
The Mouse from Longford

for Sean Cahill

PAT McCABE

WITH ILLUSTRATIONS

BY MARGOT McCABE

THE ADVENTURES OF
SHAY
MOUSE
THE MOUSE FROM LONGFORD

New Island Books / Dublin

The Adventures of Shay Mouse:
The Mouse from Longford
is published in 1994 by
New Island Books,
2, Brookside,
Dundrum Road,
Dublin 14
Ireland

Text copyright © Patrick McCabe, 1985

Illustrations copyright © Margot McCabe, 1985

ISBN 1 874597 13 8

New Island Books receives financial assistance from
The Arts Council (An Chomhairle Ealaíon),
Dublin, Ireland.

This book was first published in 1985 by The Raven Arts
Press who have originated this edition.

Cover design by Jon Berkeley
Printed in Ireland by Colour Books, Ltd.

CONTENTS

Chapter One

"YOU'RE AS WHITE AS A GHOST, SHAY MOUSE"

Shay Mouse lived in a hole in a tree in Bornacoola Wood. Well, he lived there sometimes. But most times he was to be found wandering about the wood in search of a chat, or sitting on the tree trunk beside the henhouse smoking his pipe and telling stories to young Tom Pat Badger and Mickey Slug from out by The Gap. He has plenty of yarns they loved but their favourite was the one about the time Shay Mouse beat up six rats.

— Six! Tom Pat would cry.

— Rats! Mickey would gasp, wide — eyed.

Shay Mouse would close one eye, tap the bowl of his pipe on his knee and say:

— Six rats is right. Ah what could I do? Didn't they eat up a poor bird's nest above in Tarmon? Oh I put it up to them. Eat a poor bird's nest would you? They came at me with their paws going mad in front of their auld hairy faces. In I goes bang bang bang thump bang and there they are out cold under the trees snoozin' like babies. I mean, you can't be lettin' poor innocent animals be annoyed by the likes of them.

— Oh boy, Tom Pat and Mickey would squeal, you are just so brave!

Shay Mouse didn't break his heart trying to dress himself, that's for sure. He wore a pair of battered grey trousers the whole year round and a stripey blue shirt that never had a collar. He had no wife at all. "Just meself," he said, "not another mouse in the house."

Some of the older animals told their children not to mind him, that he got "carried away". Some of them even said that it was a "pack of lies". But the young animals didn't mind what they said. They thought he was the mouse's pyjamas. Day in, day out, they gathered around him as on it went:

— I beat the ears off a cat when I was just two days old. I boxed the face off forty earwigs. I scared the daylights out of an elephant and so on. Then off he'd go, with a face on him as proud as a mouse in a poke.

But then one night in Bornacoola, a strange thing happened. It was late. Clouds moved slowly across the moon. Far away in the distance, dogs howled. Then the rumbling started. At first you could barely hear it but it grew louder and louder until the entire wood seemed to shake. Birds squawked in the trees, the ground trembled. Something terrible was happening. Eyes appeared at keyholes, faces stared from windows. Old Annie Stoat, with her shawl draped around her shoulders and the glasses shaking on her snout said: "What's going on?" Gramps Snipe, an old grouch at the best of times, grumbled: "There had better be a good reason for this." The Owl Family, Owl Sammy, Owl Johnny and Owl Jane came down from The Shaky Tree to investigate.

Then, last of all, Shay Mouse awoke. He hadn't bothered to take his clothes off so all he had to do was pop on his cap. "I'd better go and sort this out," he said to himself. There was fierce commotion in the wood now, nobody knew what was going on. Then suddenly he heard:

— Shay! Oh Shay! Come on quickly!

It was Tom Pat Badger and Mickey Slug, shaking in their night clothes.

— You must come quickly, Shay Mouse, cried Tom Pat, it's a matter of life and death!

They pulled at him to come on, he had never seen them so scared.

— Don't panic, lads, said Shay Mouse, if there's something wrong I'll sort it out. I'm in the right humour for a bit of a row, I can tell you.

— Oh Shay, I just knew you'd come in time, said Mickey, do you know what they did? They burnt out Alexis Hen and . . . kicked little Fergus!

— Burnt? gulped Shay Mouse, kicked?

— Ssh, said Tom Pat, we're here. He's starting again.

Shay Mouse could not believe his eyes. Beneath the light of the moon he could see all the animals of the wood gathered in a circle. And high up on a rock, a giant shadow was waving its paws wildly. It was . . . a . . . rat? Shay Mouse bit his lip.

And behind the rat he saw what must have been a thousand, maybe ten thousand more rats, all huddled together, squeaking and looking out of dark, wild eyes. A shiver slid down Shay Mouse's spine. As the rat roared, spits dribbled on his whiskers.

— Creatures of Bornacoola! Last week we were burnt out of our home. Fifty of our beloved comrades were poisoned because they stole a wretched ear of corn! We were burnt out of Reilly's Barn in Mullingar because we took a little food. Well, I say to you, creatures of this wood, the time for talkings'done. We have been moved on for too long. We want a home of our own — a permanent home! We rats are proud. What are we?

— Proud! shouted all the rats, their razor teeth glinting in the moonlight, proud!

— The time has come for our wandering to stop. The rat race is over! We are getting away from it all — and we have come here, to Bornacoola. It's a nice place. We like it. Fields . . . winding brown rivers . . . trees. Yes, we are fond of it. And that is why we have decided to make it our home.

The crowd gasped.

— Yes, the rat went on, we have decided to bestow on you the honour of making Bornacoola our new home. A home where we will be free from annoyance, where we shall live in peace and comfort, served by you, our loyal slaves.

The crowd went "OH!"

— Ha ha, that's a good joke, laughed Jim Worm, then went dead quiet as the rat stared straight at him.

— Yes, said the rat, from now on you will take orders from me — Pat The Rat!

— Pat The Rat, mouthed Tom Pat, barely able to speak.

— You will do everything I say, you will dance attention on all members of the Rat Regiment and then no harm will come to you. But if any of you try to get smart with me, or disobey, you will have to be eaten!

— Eaten? squealed one of the small animals and started to cry.

— Yes, that's the way its going to be from now on folks, so the sooner you get used to it the better. Tomorrow I will scrape out a set of rules for you. But in case you think life is going to be all misery under our rule, let me show you how funny, witty, wise and entertaining we rats can really be. Sebastian Rat-Smythe . . . would you be so kind as to recite your poem for the good creatures of this townland?

Another rat appeared, all shiny with twirly whiskers, looking down at the crowd as much as to say "Ugh!"

— I would be delighted, your Excellency. I would like to read you my poem, written to commemorate the night we took over Bornacoola. Namely, dim-witted animals and insects and other to-be-avoided things . . . *tonight!* My poem is called "Rhyme for Wronged Rats".

He cleared his throat delicately and began to read —

RHYME FOR WRONGED RATS

Ugly, whiskered, dirty, grey,
Bringers of disease
Long-tailed homes for homeless lice
Hotels for vagrant fleas.
Black beady eyes and filthy paws
Noses cold as ice
You see nobody likes us rats
They say we are not nice.

We live in caves and cooking pots
Sometimes in biscuit tins
Holes and walls and rivers too
And often litter bins
Nobody wants us anywhere
We do the best we can
But still old Reilly put us out
Of our beloved barn

10

So now the time for talking's done
We'll not run anymore
We're conquering this townland
To even up the score
So if you do as we rats say
We will not harm your head
But disobey us once . . . just *once*
And you will wind up dead!

Now to home you may return
My poem's at an end
Decide tonight what you will be
Enemy or friend
Sleep inside your feather bed
And don't forget who sent ya
Magnificent King Pat The Rat
The Ruler Of Rodentia!

Sebastian Rat-Smythe raised his paw in the air and cried:
— No more Bornacoola, rat brothers! Long live Rodentia.

The rats went wild, screeching and roaring Rodentia! Rodentia! Rodentia!

— Thank you, Sebastian Rat-Smythe, said Pat The Rat, as he stood up again, a fine poem indeed. Well, creatures of the wood, that's it. Bornacoola is no more. Finished. From now on its Rodentia! Do you hear? Rodentia!

A dead silence filled the wood. Then there was a creaky shout from the back of the crowd. It was GrandRobin Redbreast.

— Hey you. Hey you, Pat The Rat, he called, wobbling on his stick.

— Who dares address Pat The Rat?, boomed the voice from the rock.

— Hey you Pat The Rat, why don't you just go away and leave us in peace. We've done you no harm. You can't blame us for what happened in Reilly's Barn. Why don't you just go away and leave us in peace? We don't want you here. Go away!

Pat The Rat began to shake, his eyes were like fireballs.

— Nobody talks to me like that, bellowed Pat The Rat, nobody! Seize him!

Four rats burst forth from the squeaking thousands and grabbed GrandRobin Redbreast. They threw him down before Pat The Rat.

— You all heard this creature defy me! You all heard him insult me. I told you what happens to those who defy me! Now . . . apologise, you old fool!

GrandRobin Redbreast's voice was quivering, you could barely hear what he was saying.

— Leave us alone, he cried, we have done you no harm! Go away and leave us alone!

Mrs Redbreast ran off into the wood crying help me, help me.

— Shay Mouse, whispered Tom Pat, go on up now, go on up before anything else happens.

— Yes, Shay Mouse, said Mickey Slug, show him up for the coward he is!

Shay Mouse fiddled with the hayrope that held up his trousers.

The menacing shadow of Pat The Rat advanced. GrandRobin Redbreast tried to shout but no words came.

— Now you, grandpa, hissed Pat The Rat, I'll teach you some manners!

GrandRobin tried to cry "Go Away" but all he could manage was "geek". He began to sniffle a little bit as Pat The Rat poked and prodded him with his paws.

— Okay . . . repeat after me . . . . "I adore Pat The Rat. I am not worthy to lick his paws," commanded Pat The Rat.

— Come on Shay Mouse, said Tom Pat, when he's not looking. If you don't hurry up, there won't be time . . .

Shay Mouse said nothing, just frowned and hoped his heart would stop going so fast in his chest.

— Come on, you old fossil, boomed the voice of Pat The Rat, say it!

He curled his paws around a tattered grey wing, his eyes narrowing as he squeezed.

13

GrandRobin looked down at all the animals as if to say "I'm sorry," then in a shaky voice, said:

— I adore Pat The Rat . . . . I . . . I am not worthy to lick his paws!

Pat The Rat beamed, the rats cheered wildly. Pat The Rat shouted:

— Say it again . . . only louder this time!

The rats went "haw haw" and laughed "the auld eejit."

— Now Shay Mouse, cried Mickey.

— Come on, said Tom Pat, please!

Shay gulped and got all red.

— You're . . . you're not afraid, are you?, cried Mickey.

— Afraid? Ha Ha . . . what? Er . . . no . . . a bit sick . . . ye know like . . .

A little tear formed in Tom Pat's eye. He looked right into Shay Mouse's face.

— What's wrong, Shay Mouse? he pleaded.

The rats clutched their sides, howling with laughter as Grand-Robin repeated:

— I . . . I am not worthy to lick his paws.

— That's the stuff, you old crock! Let that be a lesson to you! snarled Pat The Rat, now — get lost!

The crowd looked on in dismay as GrandRobin Redbreast slunk off into the darkness with his old grey head hung low.

Mickey Slug started to cry. Tom Pat Badger looked away. Then Mickey said:

— You're as white as a ghost, Shay Mouse.

He paused and said bitterly:

— You didn't do anything.

— Eh?, said Shay Mouse, eh? what?

— You just stood there! You just stood there like a coward after all your big talk and all about beating up a cat and forty earwigs . . . everything you told us was lies and you're nothing but a yellabelly Shay Mouse . . . that's all you are, I hate you, I hate you! Come on away from that cowardly old fibber Tom Pat . . . let's go home.

A lump the size of a golfball came in Shay Mouse's throat

as he watched them walk away, the sound of Mickey's sobbing ringing in his ears. Then the crowd began to move away as Pat The Rat shouted:

— And let that be a lesson to you all. Off you go to your homes now . . . you have plenty of work to do tomorrow!

Shay Mouse just stood there, like he was in a dream, muttering to himself.

— What could I do, he was saying . . . he's too big . . . kill me . . . what could I do . . .

Suddenly he heard someone calling him. He froze. It was Pat The Rat himself.

— Hey you! What's your name?

— Er . . . Shay . . . Shay Mouse, said Shay.

— Where do you live . . . Shay?

— In . . . in a hole in a tree near the stile.

— Ah. That's handy. Myself and Sebastian are staying in the oil drum near the rubbish sign. Do you know it — a large red drum?

— Yes . . . Yes I do.

Pat The Rat waved a paw and called out:

— Sebastian . . . one moment please!

Sebastian came skipping across as if he were dodging tintacks.

— Yes your Excellency, most esteemed and honoured one . . . ooh what's that dreadful pong?

— This is our new neighbour, Shay Mouse.

Sebastian Rat-Smythe made a face.

— Ooh, is that so? We shall have to buy gas masks then, shan't we?

Shay Mouse's ears went red.

— Oh never mind Sebastian, Shay. He likes a little joke. Now, Sebastian . . . tell me . . what would you like for your breakfast tomorrow morning?, said Pat The Rat.

Sebastian plucked at his whiskery chin with a neat pointed nail and said:

— Let me see now . . . mm . . . some nice rotten potato skins . . . some really yukky bluemoulded bread and a soft

squashed apple. That should be rather tasty I think.

— Did you hear all that Shay Mouse? asked Pat The Rat.

— Yes . . . yes I think so, replied Shay Mouse.

— Have everything ready on the dot of eight o'clock. We don't like to be kept waiting.

Shay Mouse looked at them with his mouth open.

— But I don't understand, he said.

— He doesn't understand, said Pat The Rat.

Sebastian screwed up his face.

— He doesn't understand. The sickly smelling mouse doesn't understand. Clean out your ears mouse. Clean out your ears you ugly thing, you ugh! person!

— You are our new butler, snapped Pat The Rat, get it? You will wake us every morning, scrub our backs, press our tails, make us breakfast dinner and tea . . . and from tomorrow on you will have to leave your home in the tree. Barney Rat will live there from now on. You will move in with us. You can sleep at the end of the oil drum. Okay, mouse? Tomorrow at eight then.

Sebastian Rat-Smythe gave him another look of disgust and went off laughing and giggling with Pat The Rat.

Shay Mouse stood there for a long time. He tried to hold back the tears but he could not. Not only would all the other animals call him a coward but a traitor as well. They would say he was working for the rats to get favours for himself. There was only one thing for it. He would have to leave the wood. For ever.

He went back to his home in the tree and packed his worn old cardboard suitcase. He put in his second cap that was for Sunday wear and the toothbrush with the three hairs that his uncle in Sligo had sent to him. He lifted the picture down from the wall and read the words softly to himself — "This is my Little House" — then slipped it neatly in between his prayer-book and his reading glasses. He pulled on his overcoat and slipped out quietly. He stood by the tree for a moment and listened. By now all the creatures of Bornacoola were asleep, their dreams full of sad things, a dark and lonely silence hanging over the countryside. They saw Pat The Rat with sharp fangs and a long black whip beating all the animals viciously, Sebastian Rat-Smythe at his side, mocking and laughing cruelly. And they saw the countryside, once fresh and beautiful, turn black, withered and old. They saw the wood, once bustling and alive with happy creatures, become empty and deserted. They saw little animals dying in the fields and nobody bothering to bury them. They saw unhappiness, greed and evil.

Wiping a small tear from his eye, Shay Mouse turned and began to walk away from the wood, off down the long lonely road with his case in his hand, feeling sadder than ever before in his life.

Chapter Two

"TWO ODD CUSTOMERS"

Shay Mouse walked for hours, past strange places he had never seen before in his life, with names like Ballinalee, Newtownforbes and Longford — a huge big town where he narrowly escaped death more than once. He took the Dublin Road out of Longford and walked for about half a mile. Then he could walk no more. He nipped in behind a hedge and in seconds he was fast asleep, curled up inside a discarded tractor tyre. He had the strangest dreams — all like mixed-up pictures. Pat The Rat chased Alexis Hen through the wood with a carving knife, a tombstone read "Here lies GrandRobin Redbreast — Hero!", and long scaly fingers pointed, scary voices calling "Shay . . . Shay . . . Shay . . . "

— No, please, no! cried Shay Mouse, waking suddenly, trying to catch his breath.

Two long shadows fell over him.

— Well good day, my good fellow, said a slow, deep voice, having a little bit of a nightmare, eh? Or should I say . . . a daymare? Ha ha ha ha!

The owner of the voice grinned down at him, extending a paw.

— My name is Guy Fox. And this is my colleague, Vic Ferret. His friends all call him Fingers, don't they Fingers, ha ha ha.

— Heh heh, laughed Fingers, heh heh.

Shay Mouse uncurled himself and crawled out into the sunshine.

— How are youse doin'? My name is Shay . . . Shay Mouse.

Guy Fox wore a green waistcoat with strawberries all over it and hooked his paw into a gold watch-chain. Fingers Ferret wore a grey silk suit that had seen better days, a pork pie hat sat on his head as though it had grown there.

19

— Are youse from here? asked Shay Mouse, blinking at the light.

They looked at one another. Fingers Ferret spoke first.

— Nah, he said. Belfast, me. Him? Every place.

— Mm, smiled Guy Fox, admiring his nails, a cosmopolitian fox you might say.

— Eh? asked Shay Mouse, a what?

— I say wee mouse, said Fingers Ferret fiddling in his pocket, ye like tricks?

— Well I never seen many but I . . .

— Right, said Fingers, his paws whirling in front of his face, see these shells?

He spread three shells on the ground.

— Okay. All ye have to do is guess which one the pea is under. Here we go. La da dee dee dee yes here we go folks will he won't he yes that's what it's all about chance of a lifetime here today to win the Fingers Ferret Bonanza Shell Prize — okay mouse my friend, which shell is the pea under?

Shay Mouse took off his cap and scratched his head. He looked from one shell to the other and back again.

— I'd . . . I'd say . . . that one there, he said.

Fingers rubbed his paws.

— That one there? Right, let's see. Hey presto and what have we got. Yes sir, there you are, full of emptiness. Okay wee mouse, that's fifty pence you owe me.

Shay Mouse went white.

— But, he protested, I haven't got any money, I didn't know . . .

— Oh come on now, interrupted the Fox, don't be such an ass, Fingers, leave the poor chap alone.

— Aye, heh. Only messin' wee mouse. Only messin'. Wanna see another trick? Right — pick a card.

Shay Mouse was perplexed, he didn't know what to do.

— I don't know . . . I . . . , he said, awkwardly, who are youse?

Fingers Ferret and Guy Fox stood back in astonishment.

— You mean . . . you don't know? said Guy Fox.

— Tsk, tsk, said Fingers, he doesn't know.

— Well let's go, let's show, Fingers old friend!

— Let's jitterbug, Guy let's go go go!

Shay Mouse's eyes nearly popped out of his head at what happened next. They started dancing all around the place, Fingers Ferret doing cartwheels as Guy Fox sat on the fence singing, the pair of them waltzing and doing whirligigs of all kinds.

— Let's tell him who we are, said Guy.

— The mouse must know so away we go, said Fingers.

They joined paws and danced around him singing:

WE'RE FINGERS FERRET AND GUY FOX
WE REALLY ARE A HOWL
WE'RE NEVER SAD OR FULL OF GLOOM
YOU'LL NEVER SEE *US* SCOWL.

JOKES AND TRICKS AND PRANKS AND LAUGHS
WE'LL HAVE YOU ALL IN STITCHES
AND WHEN YOU SEE THE THREE CARD TRICK
YOU'LL NEARLY BUST YOUR BRITCHES.

HIGH WIRE ACTS AND JUGGLING
AND CYCLING ON ONE WHEEL
AND WHEN YOU SEE OUR CONJURING
YOU'LL SWEAR ITS ALL FOR REAL

SO STEP RIGHT UP DON'T BE AFRAID
ITS ALL FOR LAUGHS AND FUN
GUESS WHICH CARD IS IN MY HAND
AND WIN YOURSELF SOME MON.

SOME FOLKS THINK THAT WE ARE *BAD*
AND TRY TO FOOL OUR FRIENDS
BUT THAT'S NOT TRUE WE'RE GOOD AS GOLD
WE'RE HONEST TILL THE END.

WE'D NEVER TRY TO TRICK OR STEAL
OR RUN AWAY WITH MONEY
WE ONLY WANT TO MAKE YOU LAUGH
WITH JOKES WE HOPE ARE FUNNY.

Guy Fox nipped up neatly onto the fence like he had wings.
— Isn't that right, Fingers old friend?
— Spot on Chief, let's go with the Fingers Ferret and the Guy Fox Show.
— I say I say I say, who was that lady I saw with you last night?
— That was no lady, cried Fingers . . . that was my wife!
— Waah-haaay!, yelped Guy Fox and off they went cartwheeling again.
— Very good, old friend Fingers, cried Guy Fox, settling now in the fork of a tree . . . and now for the audience! I say I say I say what would you get if you crossed a kangaroo and a sheep?
Shay Mouse swallowed and looked about him helplessly.
— I don't know, answered Fingers Ferret, what *would* you get if you crossed a kangaroo and a sheep?
— A woolly jumper, cried Guy Fox triumphantly and then they were off again:

WE'RE FINGERS FERRET AND GUY FOX
THE LAUGH-A-MINUTE MEN
IF YOU'RE FEELING SAD OR LOW
JUST FOR US TWO SEND

WE'D NEVER BREAK INTO YOUR HOUSE
AND TRY TO STEAL YOUR MONEY
WE WOULD THINK THAT *VERY* BAD
AND NOT A SMALL BIT FUNNY.

SO NOW UNLOCK YOUR HALLWAY DOOR
DON'T HIDE YOUR POUNDS AWAY
'COS IT DOESN'T MATTER WHAT YOU DO
WE'LL GET THEM ANYWAY!

SILVER CUPS AND BAGS OF LOOT
AND PLATES OF FOOD AND TEA
WE DON'T MIND WHAT WE TAKE
AS LONG AS IT'S FOR FREE!

— Thank you F!

— Thank you G!

— What ho, old mouse, all that for free! they sang together and bowed.

It was the most amazing thing Shay Mouse had ever seen. He clapped and clapped until he was exhausted. He couldn't find the words he wanted. All he could say was:

— Janey .. bejapers!

— Glad you like it, mouse old man, said Guy Fox, fingering his watch chain.

— It was nothing, said Fingers Ferret.

— A small thing!

— But our own!

Fingers Ferret plucked a cigarette packet out of nowhere and flicked it open.

— Have a fag, mouse, he said.

— No thanks, Mr Fingers, said Shay Mouse, I don't smoke.

— Do you mind if we sit down for a wee bit?, asked Fingers.

— Not . . . not at all, said Shay Mouse. I . . . I'd be glad of the company.

— Ah that's great, said Fingers Ferret puffing on the cigarette as they sat down.

After a while sitting there listening to the sound of the birds singing and the sheep bleating, Guy Fox said:

— Tell me Shay . . . do you live here?

— No, I live in Bornacoola Wood, replied Shay.

— Bornacoola, cried Guy Fox, but that's miles and miles away!

— I know, said Shay Mouse. I . . . I had to leave it . . . for good.

Guy Fox raised an eyebrow.

— Mm, he said, interesting. Did your . . . friends come with you?

— No, answered Shay Mouse sadly, they didn't.

— So . . . so you're all on your own?

— Yes, said Shay, I'm afraid so.

— The best way to travel, said Guy Fox, on one's owney-oh, am I correct, Fingers?

— Of course, said Fingers, but of course.

There was silence for a little while and then Shay Mouse said:

— Where are youse living yourselves, men?

— Nowhere really, replied Guy Fox . . . not any more.

Shay Mouse was puzzled.

— What do you mean — not any more?

Guy Fox put his head between his paws and said in a shaky voice:

— Not since . . . not since Donald was . . . Then he started to cry.

— What's wrong? cried Shay Mouse, what's wrong, Mr Guy?

— Ssh, whispered Fingers Ferret, its better that you don't . . .

— Janey, said Shay Mouse, I'm sorry . . .

— It's all right, sniffled Guy Fox, it's all right. I'm sorry for crying like this but I get so sad when I think of him.

— Of who? Of who, Guy Fox?

— My little brother. My little furry brother, Donald.

— But what's happened him? Where is he?

— He might even be dead by now . . .

— He's not, cried Shay, he's not dead, I know it!

— He is! I know! Doody has killed him! Doody has killed my little furry red brother . . . boo hoo! boo! hoo!

— You see, explained Fingers Ferret, there's this farm up the road and its owned by Farmer Doody . . .

— And my little brother Donald has a bad heart so he has, cried Guy Fox, oh I'd love to kill that Farmer Doody!

— He keeps little animals prisoner, went on Fingers Ferret, especially little foxes, he keeps them in a hut on his farm. He does terrible things to them so he does.

— He does torture! cried Guy Fox, he tortured little Donald to death so he did!

25

— No! Shay Mouse protested, no! Maybe Donald is still alive! You can't give up hope Mr Guy!

— Do . . . do you think so?

— Yes! Maybe we could get little Donald out!

— Do . . . do you think we could?

— Yes! Yes, we could! I know we could!

— Well, let's go then, said Guy Fox, jumping up sharply, come on Fingers!

Shay Mouse did not see the sly smile that slid like a snake across Fingers Ferret's lips.

From the embankment they could see Farmer Doody's yard. And in the middle with a huge padlock on the door was Donald's prison.

— That's it, said Fingers, he has hundreds of little foxes imprisoned down there. He has them tied up with chains and ropes and he beats them with big blackthorn sticks. He makes them eat pig's food!

Shay Mouse reddened.

— I'd just love to kill that Farmer Doody! he cried.

— All you've to do Shay is stay up here behind this stone and keep your eyes peeled for Doody.

— Okay men.

— Right. Now, come on Fingers.

— Good luck men, called Shay Mouse as they crept stealthily towards the yard.

Shay Mouse's heart was pounding in his chest as he waited there watching for Doody.

— Oh I wish I knew what was happening, he said to himself, I hope Doody doesn't come out before they set little Donald free.

The minutes dragged past, he couldn't sit still. Then, out of nowhere, a snowflake settled on his nose. And then another. And another.

— Hullo. What's this? he said, don't tell me it's going to snow. At this time of year? Wait till we see . . .

26

He plucked a snowflake off his nose. Then he went as cold as ice.

— Oh no, he cried, oh no, please. It's not snow, it's not! It's feathers!

The whole place was white now, they landed everywhere.

— Hundreds of feathers! Thousands of feathers — everywhere! And they're still warm! And some of them are red! They've tricked me! Oh what have I done? What have I done!

Shay Mouse walked around in circles wondering what to do, fidgeting and talking to himself. Suddenly he broke into a run and raced across the field until he came to Farmer Doody's house. He scraped furiously at the bottom of the door until he heard Farmer Doody's voice inside.

— What's that noise? By God if it's that fox again . . .

As soon as he opened the door, Shay Mouse sank his teeth into his ankle and away with him across the field again, Farmer Doody after him with his trumpet gun. But as soon as they reached the embankment, Farmer Doody stopped in his tracks.

— My chickens! They're at my chickens!, he cried and loosed off a blast of his trumpet gun, stones, washers, bits of glass, nails and bottletops flying in the direction of the hen-house. Down below, Guy Fox let a roar out of him.

— Eek! Eek! Oh Fingers, he's got me!

— Where, where?

— On . . . on the bum! Oh Fingers!

— Oh no, cried Fingers, here he comes, run!

Guy Fox squealed like a baby and shot out of the henhouse like a bullet with Fingers Ferret after him.

— Help! Help, mammy! cried Guy Fox, my bum! Ooooh, help!

Farmer Doody stood looking after them as they disappeared into the distance.

— Go on then, he called out, go on you thieving pests! At least I got a few good shots at youse this time! And to think you would have got away with it only for this little mouse here. Where are you?

27

Shay Mouse came out from behind the gatepost.

— How can I ever thank you?

— Ah it's all right Farmer Doody. They're a bad pair of rascals so they are.

— Now you're talking. Listen. Will you come up to the house for a bite to eat . . a bit of cheese or something? Well? What do you say?

— Well, I am a bit hungry but I wouldn't like to put you out or anything . . .

— Not at all. Come on with me now and we'll give you a good dinner you won't forget in a hurry. It's not every day we meet a mouse like you . . .

Shay Mouse picked up his cardboard suitcase and followed Farmer Doody across the field, smiling happily to himself for the first time since he had left Bornacoola.

Chapter Three

"A *TALKING* LUNCH BOX?"

As Shay Mouse was tucking into a good big dinner of bread and cheese in Farmer Doody's farmhouse, some miles away a little squirrel was being brutally whacked with a sally rod. His friend, a grey squirrel looked on helplessly.

— Please don't hurt my friend, please! he pleaded.

Two cruel eyes bit into him. They belonged to Sid Swift — Honest Sid Swift, travelling showman and entrepreneur. He raised the sally rod higher.

— Then you'd better do as I say, 'adn't yer, mate? he snarled.

His wife, Nora Carbuncle, cackled evilly to herself.

— Yes, she snapped, you'll both get out there and fight and do as you are told!

— But I don't want to fight him, cried the Grey Squirrel, he's my friend!

Sid Swift lashed out with the sally rod and the Red Squirrel squealed.

— Please, no! the Grey Squirrel whimpered, I'll do as you say, I'll fight him.

Sid Swift fingered the edge of the sally rod with his wing.

— That's better, my son. Now Nora. Give these berks a bite to eat and get them out of here!

Nora Carbuncle nipped the Grey Squirrel viciously and pushed him out the door.

Of course, Shay Mouse didn't know anything about this for he was too busy eating. He ate everything Farmer Doody's wife put before him — cheese, chops, eggs, buns — he stuffed it all into him.

— Burp! he said, man that was great, then stroked his belly.

— Good Shay, said Farmer Doody, I'm glad you enjoyed it.

Do you want to sit over here in the armchair?

They sat there talking for a while and then there was a knock at the door. Farmer Doody shook his head in exasperation.

— Oh no, he said, I'd know that knock anywhere. It's that pest of an American dog that's moved into the cottage above at the Black Bridge. He has my heart scalded.

He trudged wearily to the door. A loud voice barked behind two huge swaying ears.

— Hi man, the voice said, how are ya? How ya doin'?

— Oh not so bad Zak, come on in, replied Farmer Doody. The dog stood in the middle of the kitchen. His two eyes were melting in his head, he looked like he was about to fall asleep at any moment. A banana grin hung between his floppy ears. He carried a lunch box under his arm.

— Oh Zak, I'd like you to meet Shay Mouse, said Farmer Doody.

He trailed over to Shay Mouse, his head nodding like a toy donkey in the back of a car, and held out his paw.

— Hey how are you mouse, he said, I'm Zak the Spaniel. How ya doin'?

— Er . . . not so bad, said Shay, pullin' the devil by the tail ha ha.

Zak looked at him with his mouth open.

— What, man? he said, mystified.

Farmer Doody interrupted.

— Well Zak I suppose you're looking for a few bits and pieces as usual. When are you going to get organised in that cottage?

— I don't know, man. When we came over from the States it was all gonna be really cool, us all living together, but those guys they just let the place fall down and then headed back home. Said they missed the noise man.

— Well I'll see what I can do for you so.

Farmer Doody went into the scullery.

Shay Mouse kept staring at Zak, he didn't know what to make of him and when he put the lunch box on the table and started talking to it, that snookered him altogether.

— Oh come on man, cried Zak to the lunch box, be cool.

Come outa there.

Shay Mouse swallowed. Poor Zak, he thought.

— You can't stay in a lunch box, man. You'll die. You gotta talk to people.

Shay Mouse shook his head sadly and nearly jumped out of his skin when the lunch box answered back.

— I don't care, it said, I'm staying here. So keep quiet and leave me alone, Zak!

Zak shrugged and looked at Shay Mouse.

— What's a guy supposed to do? What would you do Shay?

Shay bit his pipe stem.

— Oh now, he gulped with a bit of a laugh.

— My life's a misery with that guy.

Zak hung his head and his ears flopped around his shoulders.

— Wi. . . with who? asked Shay Mouse.

— That pigeon weirdo, man. He's been in that box for six weeks now.

— Oh . . . oh I see, said Shay Mouse, fixing his eyes on the lunch box. There was something moving about inside.

— Yes sir. Hasn't come out since the day his girlfriend Jacinta Starling left him. Just woke up one day and she was gone. Didn't even say goodbye. So he just climbed into this lunchbox and said life had no meaning, he was never coming out again.

— Oh dear, said Shay Mouse, sorry now he had doubted Zak, that's very sad.

— Sure is, said Zak, and shook his head again.

Just then Farmer Doody returned with a big brown bag.

— Well here we are Zak. There's plenty of bones and bread and stuff, should keep you goin' for a while.

— Thanks man. When I get organised and start growing my own vegetables, I'll pay you back.

Farmer Doody threw his eyes up to heaven.

— Well I guess I'll be goin', man, gotta get out on the road.

— Oh Zak, said Shay Mouse, do you think I could go a bit of the way with you? It's time I was off too.

— Sure man, nodded Zak, right on.

— You're off too? said Farmer Doody.

— I think so Mr Doody, replied Shay.

Farmer Doody held out his hand.

— Thanks for everything Shay, he said, you're a topper.

— Ah not at all, said Shay bashfully, sure I did nothing.

— Okay Shay, let's go, said Zak as he dragged himself out into the evening sunshine.

Shay Mouse walked with Zak as far as his cottage at the Black Bridge. It was a bit of a tumbledown affair, the gate was all squashed and the door hung on a hinge.

— Yeah, I gotta get it together, said Zak, I'm learning bee-keeping too.

— Is that right, said Shay, have you got many bees?

Zak screwed up his face and thought deeply.

— Well not yet man, I've just got one.

— One? cried Shay Mouse in astonishment, *one* bee?

— Right, smiled Zak sleepily, but he's gotta lotta friends.

— Well, said Shay . . . I hope it works out. I better be off so, Zak. It was nice to meet you.

— Okay Shay. And if you're ever around, call in, man. Call in and have some honey.

— Right man, said Shay Mouse, forgetting himself, then skipped off briskly down the road towards Edgeworthstown.

As he approached the town some hours later, he could hear the sound of loud cheering and clapping.

— I wonder what that could be, he said to himself.

He soon found out. Down in the hollow, a huge crowd had gathered.

— Fifty on the Grey, a voice cried.

— Seventy Five Red, Seventy Five Red!

— Twenty on the Red! Twenty on the Red lad!

A red squirrel and a grey squirrel were fighting on an orange box, urged on by the cheers of the crowd. Any time the fight slowed up, the crowd grew angry and cried "paste him," "Give

33

it to him," and "My granny could do better than that." Then the grey squirrel gave the red squirrel a punch and he fell. He managed to get up but was shaking on his legs. He looked as if he couldn't see.

— Give it to him, shouted the crowd, finish him!

— Quit holding back! Come on Grey. Get after him! Cut out the kid gloves!

The grey squirrel landed a punch on the red squirrel's jaw and he collapsed like a sack of potatoes. And then — the grey squirrel did a funny thing. He started to cry. The crowd went "BOO' and "Ah for God's sake." A rotten apple sailed into the air as someone cried "What a swiz." Then the crowd began to disperse slowly, muttering and complaining to themselves.

Shay Mouse waited until they were all gone and then he slid down into the hollow. He snook around for a bit then suddenly a cold hand fell on his shoulder. Nora Carbuncle sucked her broken black teeth as she stared down at him.

— Janey you . . . you gave me a fright, stammered Shay Mouse.

— Sid! Over here please! called Nora Carbuncle without taking her eyes off Shay Mouse, we have a visitor!

— A visitor? said Sid Swift, appearing out of nowhere, and who might he be?

— I'm Shay . . . Shay Mouse . . . I was wondering . . .

— Ye-es? said Sid Swift and Nora Carbuncle together, bending down and staring straight into his eyes.

— I was wondering if youse might have a job, like. Are youse a circus?

— Mm, I see, said Sid Swift, I see. Yes, we are a sort of circus.

— Honest Sid Swift's Travelling Roadshow, smiled Nora Carbuncle, world famous.

— So you want a job, do you? said Sid Swift, stroking his beak with his wing, but what can you do my friend?

He narrowed a black beady eye.

— Well I can sing a bit, said Shay Mouse, tell a few yarns . . .

34

— Sing, eh? Well . . . let's hear something, said Sid Swift.
Shay Mouse cleared his throat and straightened himself
up. His foot tapped as he sang:

> I'll tell me ma when I go home
> The boys won't leave the girls alone
> They pulled my hair they stole my comb
> But that's all right till I go home
> She is handsome she is pretty she is the girl
>   from Dublin City
> She is a-courtin' one two three
> Please will you tell me who is she.

He sang a couple of more verses, winking and tapping as
he went along.

— Bravo! cried Sid Swift, clapping his wings together,
bravo!

— Encore, mouse! cheered Nora Carbuncle.

— My, what a voice you've got! My goodness if we'd only
met you earlier. You'll pull them in in their thousands. Come
on, let's get something down that little tummy of yours. Tell
me . . . have you walked far?

Shay Mouse, beaming from ear to ear told Sid Swift and Nora
Carbuncle all about his travels. They sat down at a small picnic
table chatting and Shay Mouse was just going to tell them about
Farmer Doody when all the lights went out and he got a fierce
pain in his head. Far off he could hear someone laughing and a
voice saying:

"Right — in with the little pest!"

When Shay awoke, everything seemed upside down, all he
could hear was humming. Then the humming changed to a
different sound. It changed to the sound of crying. Where was
he? It was dark and he couldn't see properly.

— What's going on? he cried out.

— It's no use shouting, a small squeaky voice answered
from nearby, no-one can hear.

Shay Mouse followed the voice. There in the corner was a
small bird, a young girl bird. She was crying.

— Who are you? asked Shay Mouse, why are you crying?

— Because my life is a misery, that's why, said the bird, I'm a prisoner, boo hoo!

— A prisoner? Not at all, how would you be a prisoner?

— Can't you see? Your're a prisoner too, said the bird.

Shay Mouse went cold. He whirled around. He ran forward. Crash. Wire mesh. He tore at it, rattled it. It would not budge.

— Now do you see? Oh dear.

Shay Mouse kicked the wire in rage and nearly broke his toe.

— What's to become of us, cried the bird, we're doomed! and began to whimper anew.

— No! cried Shay Mouse, you must never give up hope! He sat down beside her and comforted her.

— Where did they get you, he asked.

— Just outside Kilashee. I went out to wash my feathers in the river and they crept up behind me. They carried me off and nobody knows where I am or anything. Boo hoo!

— Kilashee, thought Shay Mouse, no . . . it can't be . . .

— And I miss my boyfriend, she went on, and he'll think I went away or something . . .

— Yes! cried Shay Mouse, flabbergasted, it is you! Your name is Jacinta Starling, isn't it?

— Yes! Yes!, she squeaked, how did you know that?

— Because I know all about you — Zak told me!

— Zak? cried Jacinta Starling, Zak Spaniel!

— Oh we've got to get you out of here, we've got to, cried Shay Mouse excitedly.

Nora Carbuncle and Sid Swift sat around the fire counting money.

— Seven hundred and fifty one, seven hundred and fifty two, counted Sid, then he stopped sharply.

— What was that? he said.

Nora Carbuncle looked up.

They could hear the sound of shouting and rattling and banging. It got worse and worse until it became a ferocious racket altogether.

— My God if that's them animals, I'll settle their hash for them, said Nora Carbuncle, baring her dirty black teeth.

— Just make sure you don't damage them too much Nora, cautioned Sid Swift, remember the money they make us! Haw haw!

— Don't worry Sid, she replied gleefully, I've got ways and means!

She went off into the night licking her lips.

— Right, what's this then? snapped Nora Carbuncle, unlocking the cage.

— I'm not sharing a cage with a bird, cried Shay Mouse, I hate birds, I hate birds, I hate them!

Then he started running like mad around the cage, stamping his foot and roaring like a crazy mouse.

— Stop it! Stop it mouse! ordered Nora Carbuncle.

— Oh look Miss Carbuncle, look he bit me on the wing, cried Jacinta Starling.

— What? He what? shrieked Nora Carbuncle, show me!

She took her eyes off Shay Mouse for one second and that was all he needed. In a flash he had bounded out of the cage and sped off into the darkness. She screeched and screeched and screeched but it was no use. He was gone. He ran like he had propellers attached to him and soon he was pounding on Zak the Spaniel's door.

Some hours later Honest Sid Swift and Nora Carbuncle were sleeping soundly and did not hear the low drone approaching. It was like an aeroplane at night-time in the war. But they heard it all right as soon as Shay Mouse burst in the door and the air was black with bees. They bounced off the walls and windows, clouds of them settled in Nora Carbuncle's hair.

— Eek! she squealed, I'm stung!

Zak the Spaniel gave Sid Swift a good wallop on the back with the leg of a chair.

— Ouch! he cried, my back is broken!

The bees had a good time stinging the lard out of them, then

38

chased them off into the night, you could hear the squeals of them for miles.

— Right, let's get Jacinta out lads, said Shay Mouse.

— My hero! cried Jacinta Starling as she gave Shay Mouse a big smackeroo of a kiss on his nose.

— Hey man, watch it or this guy will go back into the lunch box, laughed Zak the Spaniel.

— No way Zak, laughed the lunch box pigeon, not now . . . thanks to Shay Mouse.

Shay Mouse blushed.

They stayed there laughing and talking for a good while, then Shay said:

— Well I have to be off, thanks be to God everything worked out all right.

— Gee I am sorry to see you go, Shay. Don't forget . . . you're always welcome at the cottage. I'll get in some goat's cheese especially for you, man.

Shay Mouse laughed.

— Well, goodbye everybody, he said.

They stood waving to him as he set off, a little tear glistening in the corner of Jacinta Starling's eye.

And so off he went down the road once more and that night as he slept in the boot of an old wrecked car, Shay Mouse dreamed he ran Pat The Rat and his whole Rat Regiment right out of Bornacoola.

Chapter Four

ABDUCTION!

In the days that followed, Shay Mouse walked more than he had ever done in his life, through Rathowen and Ballinalack as far as Mullingar — the home of Pat The Rat! His feet grew hard and blistered, his cap was grey and dusty. One of the buttons had popped off his braces, a single toe peeped out through his wellingtons. But on he went, past signposts, milestones, stiles and gaps. Some of the animals he met along the road would not talk to him. They said he spoke funny, pointed paws at him and said "Talk for us mouse, ha ha" and called him "Snout face". A black rabbit had said to his face: "What are you looking at, Mucky Nose?" But Shay Mouse didn't let it get him down, he just thought of all the nice animals he had encountered on his travels and knew that sooner or later things would pick up. And sure enough, as he was going down to Lough Owel one day to give himself a bit of a wash . . .

> Well — ribbit to the east!
> Ribbit to the west!
> Ribbit with my baby
> 'Cos I love you the best
>> Ribbit up!
>> Ah, ribbit up!
> Ribbit little baby, gonna ribbit the whole
>> night long!

— Thank you ladies and gentlemen, that was Sam Phibbian and The Crazy Pond Skaters singing an all-time great for you there — 'Ribbit Up!' . . . and now we'd like to follow that with one we know you all love . . . 'At The Hop!'

Shay Mouse gaped in amazement as the large green frog jumped from water lily to water lily singing at the top of his voice, tumbling the wildcat in the air. When he was finished he bowed and cried:

— Thank you! See you next week, folks!

— Bravo! cried Shay Mouse, appearing out of the undergrowth, that was great!

The frog looked embarrassed.

— Where did you come out of? he said, why didn't you let me know you were there?

— I didn't want to stop you, said Shay Mouse, you were too good.

— Oh . . . who are you anyway? A tramp mouse?

Shay Mouse winced.

— No, I am *not* a tramp mouse if you don't mind. I'm Shay Mouse from Bornacoola.

The frog smiled.

— Bornacoola, is that right? Do you know Jack Duck of the Pond there ?

— Do I what, replied Shay Mouse, I know him well. Do you know him?

— I do indeed, said the frog.

Then he paused and said:

— I suppose you have no money?

— Well I . . .

— I could give you a job for a while if you like . . . not much . . . just fixing the petals on the water lilies and a few bits and pieces like that . . .

— Oh could you? That would be . . .

— Any friend of Jack Duck's is a friend of mine. I'm Sam Phibbian. Come on and meet the folks.

— Righto, said Shay Mouse, feeling warm inside again.

Shay Mouse took the job with Sam Phibbian and spent the next few weeks having fun with the Phibbian family. They were great crack altogether. They treated him just like one of the family and even taught him how to swim. Baby Phibbian loved him. Shay Mouse fed him and his forty tadpole brothers every day. But one day as he was sitting down by the green lake mending the water lilies with dandelions and grass stalks,

41

Missus Phibbian came rushing over to him crying:

— God help us! God help us Shay Mouse! What are we going to do? Baby Phibbian went off by himself to the railway and he's been kidnapped! What are we going to do?

Sam Phibbian shook his head grimly.

One of the young woodlice that live near the sleepers told us he saw Baby Phibbian being grabbed and taken away, he said.

— But . . . by who? cried Shay Mouse, who would do that?

— Oh we know who. Cuebert Kat, that's who. He comes all the way down from Cavan to cause trouble, him and that Jubal Hopper fella that rides the earthworm. They come down here to beat up hedgehogs and torture little insects. A bad pair of rascals!

— Where do you think they've taken him?

— Back to Cavan, miles and miles away. They have a hide-out on the Longford Road.

— Oh dear.

— I've got to get after them. That Cuebert Kat will do terrible things to him so he will. He tied one of the thrushes of The Bendy Tree to a gate and left him there for three days. Then him and Jubal Hopper threw him into a river. I've got to get going . . .

— I'll go with you Sam, said Shay, there's two of them . . .

— Oh would you Shay? Would you?

— We've no time to lose, said Shay Mouse.

They waved goodbye and set off, Shay Mouse with a dock-leaf knapsack full of food on his back; Sam Phibbian scouting on ahead, the eyes moving right around in his head. They walked for miles and miles and were just beginning to get tired when they heard voices. Below in the quarry, a stoat dressed in top hat and tails was standing on top of a tin hut making a speech of some kind.

— Animals, vegetables, minerals, he cried, lend me your ears. Some of you well know how cold it is going to be this winter. For those of you who don't, let me tell you here and now that

ABDUCTION!

it will freeze the fur off you. And that is why I, Wesley Stoat, am offering you my new invention — ear wigs, folks! Yes, genuine, insulated ear wigs, guaranteed to keep you warm as toast the whole winter long! Step right up now!

Shay Mouse and Sam Phibbian waited until they had all gone and Wesley Stoat was packing his things, then they went down to the hut.

— Hello, said Sam Phibbian.

— Hello there, brothers, come to buy something, eh? What about a tail-curler for you young mouse? Or a tooth sharpener? And you frog friend . . . some Sta-Stik for your tongue perhaps?

— No, said Sam Phibbian, thanks all the same, but we're looking for someone.

— Oh? Who?

— Jubal Hopper and Cuebert Kat. They've kidnapped my son.

— Kidnapped! Good Lord! Does one of them ride an earthworm?

— Yes, that's him!

— I saw him about two hours ago! They're heading towards Cavan!

— Let's get going Shay. Thank you Wesley, said Sam Phibbian.

— But before you go, what about this week's Special Offer? Tins of Snarlfood at half-price! Extra strong! Dogs love it. Never late for tea, they can smell it for miles. Well?

— No thanks Wesley, said Sam, we must be . . .

— Ah sure give us a few tins, said Shay, on account of you helping us . . .

— Very good little mouse . . . three be enough?

Shay Mouse nodded and slipped the three tins into his pack. They thanked Wesley Stoat and set off once more.

It was getting dark as they approached Legan and Sam Phibbian said:

— They can't be too far ahead of us now . . . I'll call in and

44

see if my friend James J. is in. He might know something.

The sign on the tree read:

JAMES J. HOGG,
SPINE MERCHANT
LEGAN.

A grey hedgehog in tattered clothes and cracked spectacles answered their knock.

— Yes? he said wearily.

— It's me, Sam Phibbian, said Sam.

— Oh . . . Sam! do come in . . .

— And this is my good friend, Shay Mouse, added Sam Phibbian.

— Hello my good fellow, said James J., tripping over the step.

Inside was like a cave, all dark and musty. There were hedgehog spines everywhere, dangling from the ceiling and hanging on the walls. Notices read:

SPINES MENDED, 10p
SIX PACK OF SPINES, £2.50

— Do you fix spines, James J? asked Shay Mouse.

— What's that Fred? answered James J., now where's the teapot?

— That's a bucket, said Sam, here let me do it . . .

James J. scratched his snout.

— Spines? Yes, yes I do. 10p each.

— And you sell them too?

— Yes.

— Only in six packs?

— No no. Ones as well. 40p each.

— Could I have one please? asked Shay Mouse.

— But of course Jim, was the reply.

Shay Mouse wrapped up the spine in his pack. He liked to keep souvenirs of places. At tea, James J. said he had seen the kidnappers all right but he couldn't remember if it was yesterday or two years ago. Sam Phibbian sighed.

— Well, he said, we'd better be off.

— So soon? said James J.

— We've no time to lose James, but we'll call again.

45

James J. saw them to the door.

— Don't forget to call again Sam. And good luck George Mouse.

Shay Mouse shook his head.

Out on the road once more, Sam Phibbian said to Shay:

— It was good of you to buy that spine. He doesn't do much business any more. They all go to the new Spinemarket in Longford.

— Oh you never know when it'll come in handy, said Shay Mouse.

Night fell suddenly as they made their way along the Granard Road.

— Ssh, said Sam Phibbian, stopping dead in his tracks, what was that? Did you hear that Shay?

They stood in the middle of the road with their ears pricked up. It was the sound of singing, not far away. Slowly, stealthily, they went around the bend. A red glow lit up the sky. Now they could hear the singing plainly:—

> Well I'm a mean grasshopper
> Ah kill me baby frawgs
> And when I'm finished killin'
> Ah throw them to the dawgs
> YIPPEEE! Gonna die, baby!

— Suffering Flip, cried Shay Mouse, its them!

Jubal Hopper sat beside a campfire singing away. His worm was tethered to a blade of grass. Cuebert Kat, his eyes mad and red, was dancing like an indian around the place, shouting and roaring. And there, tied to a dandelion, was Baby Phibbian.

— Look at Phibbian, yelled Cuebert Kat, the auld green skin of him. Scared, aren't ye Phibbian? Where's your daddy now? Hur hur hur!

— I'll kill that Cuebert Kat, cried Sam Phibbian, the eyes jumping in his head.

47

— No, said Shay Mouse, wait till they get tired . . . I have a plan . . .

— They waited for about two hours and then at least, Jubal Hopper rose and stretched himself.

— Waal, he said, I guess I'll turn in, Cuebert ol' pard.

— Right ye hopper ye, I think I will meself, was the reply.

Some time later, Sam Phibbian and Shay Mouse crept down to Baby Phibbian.

— Boo hoo, boo hoo, wept Baby Phibbian, I want my daddy!

— Ssh, whispered Sam Phibbian, don't make a croak, I'm right behind you. Ssh.

He untied the straw around the little thin legs and they slipped back into the undergrowth. Meanwhile Shay Mouse scuttled over to the two sleeping figures, silent as a mouse with tea cosy shoes. Slowly he opened the tins of Snarlfood that Wesley Stoat had sold him and carefully emptied the contents all around them. The he unwrapped the large spine and pinned the two of them to the ground by their shirts so that they couldn't move. Without a sound he slid back into the darkness and hid behind a tree. Cuebert Kat woke up first, sniffing.

— Huh? Huh? Whassa matter? Ugh! Such a stink! Hi Jubal, what's that smell? Is that smell comin' off you? Hi quit pullin' me, Hopper!

— *Me* pulling *you!* I ain't pullin' nobody! You got it wrong, pard. YOU'RE pulling me!

— Come on now, snapped Cuebert Kat, quit actin' the eejit, you're pullin' me and that's all's about it! Well I'm tellin' ye, I'm not in the humour for it, so ye can quit it.

— Look here yuh sidewinder . . .

— Leave off . . .

Then a dogbark echoed, far away. Then another dogbark.

— What was that?

— Quit changin' the subject! Let me up!

And another dogbark. And another. They came from all directions. Suddenly out of the darkness sprang a little red terrier . . . followed by a huge oily Alsatian!

— Dogs! squealed Jubal Hopper, help!

— I hate dogs, yelled Cuebert Kat, they'll ate me!

Now there was nothing only dogs — big ones, small ones, black ones, red ones.

— Aaagh! they bit me, cried Jubal Hopper.

— There's somethin' stuck here Hopper . . . a needle or somethin' . . . pull it out, quick!

Jubal Hopper pulled with all his might and out came the spine, ripping their shirts into shreds as it did. The dogs pawed and licked at them to get the Snarlfood. A Doberman Pinscher took a right bite out of Cuebert Kat.

— Let me out of here! he squealed, I'm destroyed!

— Wait for me! cried Jubal Hopper.

All you could hear then was the sound of them running away screeching:

— Please don't bite us dogs, please . . . we're sorry ow! ow! ow!

The dogs licked up what was left of the Snarlfood and went off once more into the night.

— Oh daddy, cried Baby Phibbian, thank you for coming to save me! They did terrible things to me! They said they were going to kill me!

— There there Baby, you're in safe hands now, you've nothing more to worry about. But it's not me you have to thank son. The person you have to thank is old Shay Mouse. Without him, I don't know what I'd have done.

Shay Mouse looked at the ground, a little red.

— Oh thank you Shay Mouse, thank you thank you thank you!

— Well we'd best be off, said Sam Phibbian, we've a long walk ahead of us.

He put his arm around Shay Mouse and Baby Phibbian and they set off down the road and that night Shay Mouse dreamed that Pat The Rat and Sebastian Rat-Smythe, dressed in rags, brought him his dinner on a golden plate and said: "Will that be all, your Excellency?"

49

Chapter Five

"THE BOOT'S ON THE OTHER PAW NOW, SEBASTIAN!"

All that summer Shay Mouse stayed with the Phibbian family helping out with the household chores, taking Baby Phibbian for long walks in the evening sunshine. But then, when the brown leaves were beginning to fall from the trees and the crops ripening in the fields, he decided it was time to move on.

— Are you sure you won't stay for another while Shay?, asked Sam Phibbian.

— No Sam, he replied. I'd better be movin' on. Thanks for everything. You've been very good to me. Goodbye!

He set off down the road once more, already wondering what new adventures were in store for him. He took a lift a good part of the way in a haycart and found himself on a road bigger than any he had every seen in his life. Cars whizzed past, lorries roared and threw dust in his face. Motorbikes spluttered. The noise almost deafened him. By the time he saw the lights of a new town, he was exhausted. But this was an unusual town. The lights stretched away across the sky, they seemed to go on forever. The buildings reached far up into the clouds. Night was falling, people hurried through the streets. Shay Mouse noticed a strange thing. Nobody spoke. Nobody at all. A man stood at a street corner ranting and raving to himself about the end of the world. Two men got out of their cars and beat each other up on the sidewalk. Small children with dirty faces and sweetboxes asked people for money. Shay Mouse left down his suitcase and sat on a step watching it all. The grey tired faces pushed past in the drizzling rain. He wished one of them would stop and talk. But nobody did. He got up again, drifted through the wet streets, cold and tired, trying to think of things that would make him happy. He tried to think of Zak and Farmer Doody and Jacinta

Starling and the talking Lunch Box . . . but his mind kept going back to the wood in Bornacoola, to the sad faces of his friends Tom Pat Badger and Mickey Slug and GrandRobin Redbreast waving his wing at Pat The Rat.

— I don't care about the rats, he cried aloud, forgetting himself, I want to see my friends! I want to see Tom Pat and Mickey. I don't like it here so I don't! I hate this smoke and noise!

He looked up to see a mouse in a blue denim jacket and a bristly head standing above him tapping his foot.

— Hey John, said the mouse, you all right dere?

— Er yes, I'm all right, answered Shay Mouse.

— You looked a bit pale there for a minute. My name's Manky. Manky Mouse. Gorra cigarette?

— Er . . . no. I don't smoke.

— Wha? Givvis tenpence then.

— I'm afraid I haven't got any money . . .

— Where are you from? Down the country?

— Yes . . .

— Whereabouts? Kerry?

— No. Bornacoola.

— Wha? What kind of a name is that? Whatcha got in that case?

— Not much . . . just an old coat and a . . .

— I think you have money . . .

— I haven't. I have nothing.

— Are you calling me a liar? snapped the mouse, moving in closer.

— No . . . I just want to . . .

— Listen, John, I don't like being called a liar. Now let's have a look in that case . . .

He pulled at the case roughly.

— Come on! Give it to me! Give me it, you thick!, he snarled.

— No, please! Help, leave it alone! cried Shay Mouse.

The mouse pulled and tugged at it. Shay Mouse was white, he didn't know what to do. Then he heard a deep growl. The

mouse let go sharply and jumped back. A black and white dog leaped down on them.

— Well Manky, my old pal, up to your tricks again, eh? How are things in Ballybough? Giving you trouble, is he, mouse?

— No Larry, quaked Manky Mouse, only having a birrov a mess like . . .

— Right. Now get on your bike and beat it. And tell Razor and Tomo we're looking for them . . .

— R . . . right Larry, sure, said Manky Mouse and bolted down the street as fast as he could.

— Th . . . thanks very much, said Shay Mouse, you saved me. I don't know what's going on. I can't get used to this place at all.

— Where are you from? asked the dog.

— Bornacoola.

— Isn't that outside Longford?

— Yes, cried Shay Mouse excitedly, do you know it?

— No, but my cousin Jack does. He's from Mullingar. Why don't you come and meet him?

— God aye, said Shay Mouse.

The dog held out his paw.

— I'm Larry. Larry the Ringsend Terrier.

— Shay. Shay Mouse.

Larry's kennel was in a backyard in Ringsend. As they came through the gate, they heard snarling and snapping and barking.

— You dirty rat! growled the voice, I'll kill you! I'll tear you to pieces! I hate rats, I hate rats, I hate them!

Larry told Shay not to be afraid and called out:

— Hey Jack . . . I brought a friend home . . .

The dog looked around with his eyes narrowed.

— What?, he said, *tonight?* The night of *Operation Meaty Chunks?*

— Oh come on Jack. He was stuck. Anyway maybe he can come along.

— Oh all right, sighed the dog. Just annoyed I missed that filthy disease carrier. Come on in, men.

53

Jack Russell and Larry The Ringsend Terrier made Shay Mouse a good dinner and filled him a big bowl of water for afters.

— Well, said Jack, its good to meet somebody from down that way Shay . . .

— Why did you leave Mullingar yourself, Jack? asked Shay Mouse.

Jack Russell looked away, Larry frowned.

— After, Jack Russell began, after my father died. After I saw him torn to bits by rats outside a barn. He hadn't a chance. Thousands of them. I swore I'd avenge him. I've looked everywhere for them. But then, when we were searching, my brother Jack was lifted and taken off in a van to *Sunny Meadows Dogs' Home* in Ballsbridge. But . . . but what's wrong Shay Mouse? You've gone very pale . . .

Shay Mouse could hardly speak.

— Was . . . was one of the rats a great big fellow with whiskers the size of car aerials and claws like knives? And another fella all shiny with twirly whiskers?

— Yes . . . yes but . . .

— I know them! cried Shay Mouse excitedly, they're in Bornacoola. They took it over and made the animals into slaves! They're in Bornacoola Jack! I can take you to them!

— At last! At last my prayers are answered! Oh thank you, oh thank you for coming here tonight Shay Mouse!

— Now, said Larry the Ringsend Terrier, all we have to do is get Jack out of *Sunny Meadows* . . .

— Phyllis dear, called the owner of *Sunny Meadows Excelsior Dogs' Home*, could I have some more "Chuck-a Bye Byes" food for little Rex here please?

— Yes, answered Gladys, her sister, but of course dear. Now . . . here we are.

— Eat it up, said Phyllis to the little dog, expensive food for the dear poopsy whipkins!

Two two women cackled. They both looked exactly the same. They wore pink dresses with pineapples and palm trees all over them and glasses with wings.

— I don't like it, whimpered the little dog, it's full of stones and bits of coal . . .

Gladys snarled.

— Why, you ungrateful little pup! Don't like it! Just you wait until your new owner Doctor Josef Klein gets you! Don't like it indeed! Well let me tell you my cheeky young friend! I'll teach you some manners! Phyllis . . . could you hand me the "Manners" stick please?

— Certainly dear, said Phyllis, taking down a long thin cane with a crooked handle.

— Now . . . hold out your paw, snapped Phyllis.

— P . . . please, not hard, pleaded the little dog.

Phyllis gave him six hard whacks with the cane and pushed his nose down into the food bowl.

— Now. Let that be a lesson to you, you cheeky mongrel, she said viciously.

— He'll not be so quick to refuse food the next time, cackled Gladys, I must remember to put a few little pieces of glass in it . . .

Outside *Sunny Meadows* all was quiet. Or so it seemed.

— Are you ready Shay? whispered Jack Russell, you're sure you'll be able to go through with it?

— Sure Jack, said Shay Mouse . . .

— Right . . . go!

Shay Mouse sped through the darkness. He scuttled up the wall and down the other side. Now for the door. He squeezed and squeezed underneath, just another little bit . . . that's it . . .

Phyliss looked up from the knitting pattern in her *Woman's Weekly*.

— Gladys? Did you hear something? she said.

— Why no, came the reply, I . . .

Shay Mouse squeaked loudly.

— Look! cried Phyllis, over there Gladys . . .

— Ugh! It's a mouse! Filthy mice! Let's get him and kill him!

— No Gladys! Don't surprise him! He might get away! Wait. Here little mousey. Do you want some cheese? Here little mouse. I'll get you some cheese.

Shay Mouse sank his teeth into her finger as hard as he could. She squealed.

— Ow! Ow, Gladys! He bit me! Get him! Show no mercy!

Shay Mouse tore out of the room with Phyllis and Gladys after him. He squeezed beneath the door . . .

— Look, he's getting out under the door . . . Open it Gladys! cried Phyllis, sucking her finger.

The bolt of the door flew back and in bounded Jack Russell and Larry The Ringsend Terrier.

— Get off me you filthy mongrels, shrieked Phyllis, get away from my leg! Gladys, do something!

— Oh please, oh please dogs, we'll do anything, whimpered Gladys, we don't mean to harm little dogs, we don't sell them for money or anything, honest we don't ow ow ow!

— Just open the kennels you tyrants! barked Jack Russell, and quick!

— Oh dear, they cried, and shuffled off with the keys.

Soon *Sunny Meadows Dogs' Home* was alive with happy barking dogs of all kinds and Phyliss and Gladys were each squashed into a kennel of their own, staring out hopelessly. Jack Russell stood on a carboard box marked '2 by 15 USED CHUNKY BITS' and made a speech.

— You are all free to go, he said. You'll never have to worry about these two or *Sunny Meadows* again. But I have one favour to ask. I need volunteers for a special mission! We are off tomorrow to free Bornacoola from Pat The Rat and his Rat Regiment. We are off to free Bornacoola from the killers of my father. Any dog who wishes to join us let him bark now! What about these two Kerry Blues here?

— By God, I'll go, said one.

— Sure ting, boy, said the other.

— And me! cried a Red Setter.

— I can't wait to get at them, called a Pointer.

— We'll all go, shouted everybody, waving paws and ears excitedly.

— Great stuff! said Jack Russell. We can spend the night at my place. We march on Bornacoola tomorrow!

— Bornacoola, they cried, and fell in behind Jack Russell, Larry and Shay Mouse.

At cock crow the following morning, the dog army was lined up and ready to move.

— Companee! Ten-shun! commanded Jack Russell, saluting.

— Now . . . we must all be careful! Stay off the main roads and don't do anything that might attract attention! Shay . . . over to you.

Shay Mouse cleared his throat and stood up.

— We'll all meet at the old castle on the edge of Bornacoola. We'll not do a thing until we're all there. We'll discuss the plan then. Okay?

The dogs barked in unison.

— Companee! Fall out! And may God go with you, said Jack Russell.

The dogs shot off down the road. Shay Mouse, Jack Russell and Larry gathered up their belongings and set off on the long march to Bornacoola Wood.

A fat yellow moon hung in the sky above the ruined castle outside the wood as the army waited patiently for everyone to arrive. Shay Mouse paced up and down anxiously. Dogs scurried through the undergrowth and whispered.

— It's me. I'm here.

Shay saluted and nodded. Jack Russell sat on a tree trunk thinking deeply. Time passed slowly. Then Shay Mouse said:

— Well men. It looks as if everyone's here. Now, listen carefully . . .

An eerie silence descended on the wood. The dark leaves rustled in the trees, clouds moved slowly in the red sky. Somewhere an owl hooted. Then, deep in the wood, a voice cried out:

— Pat The Rat is a filthy rodent!

And then another voice —

— Did you hear that Pat The Rat?

— Pat The Rat is brutal and ugly!

— Pat The Rat tortures helpless creatures!

— Pat The Rat is not wanted here!

In the oil drum Pat The Rat woke with a start. Sebastian Rat-Smythe was still sleeping soundly. Pat The Rat hit him a thump.

— Smythe! Smythe! Wake up you fool! Did you hear that?

— What? What? said Sebastian with his eyes all scrunched up.

The voices began again.

— Pat The Rat is a filthy rodent!

— Clean your whiskers Pat The Rat!

Pat The Rat was ready to blow up with fury. He jumped out of bed calling:

— Assemble the guards! I want all rats on duty! I'll make them sorry for this! I'll kill every creature in the wood! To your posts, rats!

Rats raced out of rivers, holes, trees and buckets.

Pat The Rat stood menacingly in the middle of the wood.

— Wherever you are, he ordered, you had better come out. If you don't we'll come in after you! This is your last chance! I'll count to three and if you're not out by then I'll . . . one . . . two . . . three . .

Shay Mouse nipped out from behind a tree.

— Hello, he said coolly, hello Pat the Rat.

Pat The Rat could not believe his eyes. He looked at Shay

59

Mouse for a moment with his mouth open, then burst into laughter.

— Ha! ha! Look who it is Sebastian! The stupid old mouse who was going to be our butler.

— Tsk! Tsk! sneered Sebastian Rat-Smythe, the cheek of the disgusting, smelly old thing!

— Look who it is men, said Pat The Rat, an old mouse! A stupid old mouse!

The rats squeaked their heads off with laughter. Pat The Rat's face grew dark and evil.

— Get ready to die, mouse, he said in the same voice he had threatened GrandRobin Redbreast.

— Oh, Pat The Rat? said Shay Mouse, yawning and examining his nails.

Pat The Rat stopped in his tracks.

— Yes? he said, frowning.

— I'd like you to meet my friend, Jack Russell.

— Jack Russell leaped out from the undergrowth snarling viciously, teeth bared.

— Ja . . . Jack Russell? gulped Pat The Rat, then moved back.

— Yes! snapped Jack Russell, that's right. You and your rats killed him! He was my father!

— N . . . n . . . now wait a minute, stammered Pat The Rat, I . . . I . . . can explain . . .

— It's too late for that, *you dirty rat!* Now men!

— Geronnnimooooooo! yelled Larry, racing down the hill with hundreds of dogs after him.

— Come on men, shouted Shay Mouse, now we have them!

— Help mammy! cried Sebastian Rat-Smythe.

— Yee-haa! yelled Larry, running past with a rat in his mouth.

Dust rose in the air, the sound of the fighting filled the sky. On it went, far into the morning, bodies littering the ground, faces torn and bleeding. Jack Russell and Pat The Rat fought on, snarling spitting, clawing, until at last, barely able to stand, Pat the Rat cried weakly:

— I can't fight anymore! I can't go on. The battle is over! We . . . surrender!

— Hooray! cried all the animals of the wood, appearing from their homes, hooray, hooray, horray!

They had a feast to end all feasts that day. And when the eating was over, Shay Mouse stood up at the head of the table. Everybody clapped and cheered.

— Thank you, he said. Thank you everybody. Now I have here beside me someone you all know well — Sebastian Rat-Smythe. Some time ago Sebastian read a poem for us called 'Rhyme for Wronged Rats'. He has a new one for us now. What's it called, Sebastian?

Sebastian Rat-Smythe hung his head in shame.

— It's called 'Ballad of Beaten Brutes', he said.

Jim Worm shouted up from the audience:

— Ha ha! The boot's on the other paw now, Sebastian!

— Away you go, Sebastian, said Shay Mouse.

Sebastian began to read in a shaky voice:

BALLAD OF BEATEN BRUTES

ONE NIGHT IN NINETEEN EIGHTY FOUR
WHEN ALL CREATURES SLEPT IN BED
THE MOON SHONE HIGH UP IN THE SKY
THE CLOUDS WERE COLOURED RED
THROUGH THE UNDERGROWTH THEY CAME
A SOUND THEY DID NOT MAKE
NOT ONE CREATURE HEARD THEM COME
AND SO DID NOT AWAKE.

THEN THE SKY GREW DARK AND GREY
STRANGE SOUNDS FILLED THE WOOD
A RUMBLING ROLLING SOUND LIKE DRUMS
THE POUNDING OF RED BLOOD.

HIS UGLY VOICE IT FILLED THE AIR
AND WHIRLED ABOUT THE TREES
HIS NAME IT WAS KING PAT THE RAT
THE BRINGER OF DISEASE.

THEN THE HAPPY DAYS THEY WENT
THEY FADED FAR AWAY
NO LAUGHTER ECHOED ANYMORE
ALL WAS SAD AND GREY.
NO GAMES WERE PLAYED OR STORIES TOLD
NO SUN SHONE IN THE SKY
AND BY THE SIDE OF DUSTY ROADS
OLD CREATURES WENT TO DIE.

NOTHING HAPPENED ANYMORE
TREES HUNG DOWN THEIR LEAVES
NO ONE REMEMBERED ANYMORE
THE DAYS BEFORE THE THIEVES.
THEN ONE DAY THE LIGHT GREW BRIGHT
THE SUN CREPT OUT FROM CLOUDS
AND HIGH UP IN THE HEAVENS
BIRDS CALLED A NAME ALOUD.

"SHAY MOUSE", THEY CHIRPED IN EVENSONG
SHAY MOUSE RETURNS AGAIN
HE'S COME TO HELP THE CREATURES HERE
AND BROUGHT ALONG HIS FRIENDS.
"RISE UP," HE CRIES, I'LL SHOW YOU HOW
AT LAST WE'LL SHOW THESE BRATS
AND NEVER MORE BE THREATENED BY
THESE ROTTEN, RANCID RATS!

AND SO THE RATS WERE BEATEN
AND MADE TO EAT THEIR WORDS
NO MORE THEY'LL TORTURE LITTLE MICE
AND STROLL AROUND LIKE LORDS
THEIR TYRANT DAYS ARE AT AN END

THEY'RE WEARING CONVICT SUITS
NO MORE WE'LL FEAR OR SHED A TEAR
FOR THESE BROKEN, BEATEN BRUTES.

— Three cheers for Shay Mouse, Jack Russell cried.
— Pat the Rat is dead! Long live Bornacoola!
Shay Mouse raised his paw in the air. The cheers of all the animals shook the wood.
Sebastian Rat-Smythe slunk off, his once twirly whiskers hanging down now and his coat all bald and raggy.

Shay Mouse said goodbye to Larry and Jack and all the dogs and thanked them once more for their help. He stood watching as they marched off into the distance and then, putting his paws around the shoulders of his two young friends, Tom Pat Badger and Mickey Slug, he walked back to the wood where the starlings were singing sweetly in the trees. He went to his little home and collected his pipe and then they went to sit on the tree trunk beside the henhouse.

They sat there until the sun was sinking low behind the distant hills and as they listened to the exciting stories of his travels far beyond Bornacoola, Tom Pat Badger and Mickey Slug knew that they were listening to the bravest mouse in the whole wide world.